Weekend Comedy

by
Jeanne Bobrick
and
Sam Bobrick

A SAMUEL FRENCH ACTING EDITION

SAMUEL
FRENCH
FOUNDED 1830

New York Hollywood London Toronto

SAMUELFRENCH.COM

IMPORTANT BILLING AND CREDIT REQUIREMENTS

All producers of WEEKEND COMEDY *must* give credit to the Author of the Play in all programs distributed in connection with performances of the Play and in all instances in which the title of the Play appears for purposes of advertising, publicizing or otherwise exploiting the Play and/or a production. The name of the Author *must* also appear on a separate line, in which no other name appears, immediately following the title, and must appear in size of type not less than fifty percent the size of the title type.

WEEKEND COMEDY was first presented in 1985 at Tiffany's Attic in Kansas City, MO by Dennis D. Hennessy and Richard Carrothers.

A 1986 production at Stage West in Calgary, Canada, starred the following cast:

Frank...........................George Kennedy

Peggy.............................Dodie Brown

Jill.............................Shannon Kennedy

Tony..............................Peter Yunker

Directed by
Sam Bobrick

CHARACTERS

FRANK & PEGGY . . . . . . A couple in their early fifties.

JILL & TONY . . . . A couple in their mid twenties.

TWO ACTS

ONE SET

ACT ONE

Scene One

TIME: Late Friday afternoon of a Memorial Day weekend.

The play takes place in the main room of a comfortable two room upstate New York vacation cabin. Stage Right is the front door. Stage Left is a door to the bedroom. In the room is a kitchen and eating area, several windows, a fireplace, a sofa bed, several chairs, tables and lamps, typical of what you'd expect in such a cabin. A suitcase is in the middle of the room, and there are several boxes of groceries on the counter.

The front door opens and FRANK JACKSON enters. FRANK is a man in his early fifties. He is wearing a dress shirt with no tie, suit pants, a cardigan sweater and loafers. This is the extent of FRANK's sports clothes. He is carrying a couple of wet logs. One of his knees has a fresh mud spot on it.

FRANK. *(calling towards bedroom)* Peggy! *(There is no response. He starts towards the fireplace.)* These logs are too damn wet. I'll never get them started. *(On the cross, one of the logs falls on his toe.)* Damn! *(He hops the rest of the way to the fireplace with one foot.)* Damn! Damn! Damn! Damn! Damn! Damn! *(He sets the logs in the fireplace, limps over to the log he has dropped, picks it up, returns to the fireplace and speaks to the log before throwing it in.)* I'm glad I'm burning you. *(He throws the log in.)*

(PEGGY JACKSON comes out of the bedroom. PEGGY is a nice looking woman in her late forties. She is wearing a beautiful penoire. She models it for FRANK.)

PEGGY. What do you think, Frank?

FRANK. What do I think about what?

PEGGY. About what I'm wearing?

FRANK. Are you going to take a nap already?

PEGGY. That's what I love about you, you're so romantic.

FRANK. How can I be romantic! I almost broke my neck out there falling in a hole. Look what I did to my favorite pants.

PEGGY. Frank, you've had those pants for ten years. Do yourself a favor. Throw them in the fireplace and don't look back.

FRANK. Are you crazy? They're polyester. The fumes would kill us... Peggy, you should see it outside. There must be twenty holes out there. I hope to hell there's not a bear digging them. That's all I need is to come face to face with a bear.

PEGGY. Well, if you do, think of it as the bear's problem.

FRANK. Why I let you talk me into coming up here, I'll never know. Did you ever stop to think what would happen if one of us had an appendicitis attack?

PEGGY. I had mine out when I was ten.

FRANK. Great. That leaves me.

PEGGY. Hey, why don't we sit down and have a beer.

FRANK. *(indicating suitcase)* What about that last bag?

PEGGY. I unpacked the bag with your shirts, I unpacked the bag with your pants. I unpacked the bag with your socks and underwear ... *(Lifts suitcase.)* This one is the bag with your extra shirts, pants, socks and underwear. I'll unpack it when we get home.

FRANK. You think I took too much, don't you?

PEGGY. No. Not if we go straight from here to Europe for seven months. You get the beer. *(She takes the suitcase into the bedroom.)*

FRANK. *(Takes two beers from a packed refrigerator.)* By the way, I like that outfit you're wearing a lot, but maybe you'd better change into something more practical. I mean, I wouldn't want you to catch cold.

PEGGY. *(coming out of bedroom)* Frank, I'm not going to catch cold and you're not going to have an appendicitis attack. We're going to have three lovely days together in spite of the fact that since we left the city, you have been a tremendous pain in the ass.

FRANK. *(Hands her a can of beer.)* Is that right?

PEGGY. Lighten up, Frank. For once in your life enjoy yourself.

FRANK. Do I have to?

PEGGY. You have to. *(Gets two glasses for them and pours the beer.)* Let's not worry about anything this weekend ... about the business, about the kids, about baseball ... Let's just forget everything. Just you and me.

FRANK. Okay. Okay. If that's what you really want ... for me to be unhappy, I'll try.

PEGGY. What a great guy!

FRANK. Thank you. *(He sits on the sofa.)*

PEGGY. You know why I rented this place?

FRANK. You told me. No telephone.

PEGGY. *(Snuggles next to him.)* No telephone, no television, no newspaper.

FRANK. No newspaper? You didn't tell me there was no newspaper.

PEGGY. There're about six houses up here in twenty miles. Who's going to have a paper route?

FRANK. My luck, there's finally going to be some good news and I'll miss it.

PEGGY. The good news is that this is our first time alone in ages. This is our first real vacation in years.

FRANK. *(a little hurt)* Oh, come on. Wasn't that week in St. Louis a vacation?

PEGGY. Frank, no week in St. Louis is a vacation. Besides, we were there to see the new line of office supplies. It was business.

FRANK. Of course, it was business. How else can you deduct a vacation?

PEGGY. Promise me something, okay? Promise me that while we're up here I won't have to hear one word about typewriters, stationery or that the paper they're using for next year's calendars is real crap. I want you to spend time with me. I want us to spend time together.

FRANK. Up here?

PEGGY. That's right.

FRANK. Just you and me.

PEGGY. Uh huh.

FRANK. With nothing to do.

PEGGY. *(romantically)* Maybe you'll think of something.

FRANK. All we can do is eat and have sex.

PEGGY. Now you got it.

FRANK. I'm not hungry.

PEGGY. What about choice B?

FRANK. You want to have sex?

PEGGY. Why not? Some people think it's fun.

FRANK. Who?

PEGGY. Frank, if you want to leave here alive you'd better be teasing.

FRANK. You really want to fool around?

PEGGY. To be more specific, why don't you throw me on the sofa, rip off my clothes and fulfill your needs.

FRANK. Have you been unpacking our clothes or reading a dirty book?

PEGGY. Do you really love me?

FRANK. Of course. Don't I let you share my razor?

PEGGY. *(rises)* I'm locking myself in the bedroom.

FRANK. *(Grabs her.)* Come here!

PEGGY. Leave me alone, Frank. I'm going to try to be mad.

FRANK. Get back here. I'm about to be romantic.

PEGGY. Too late.

FRANK. I must have you. *(PEGGY tries to break away, but FRANK forces her to the ground.)*

PEGGY. Frank...

FRANK. *(on top of her, kissing her)* Well, what do you think of me now?

PEGGY. I'm not so sure. Give me another sample.

FRANK. *(Kisses her again.)* Well?

PEGGY. If my husband ever catches me with you....

FRANK. You know what we're going to do this weekend?

PEGGY. Tell me?

FRANK. Screw! All day, all night. In that room, in this room...

(As FRANK continues talking, TONY and JILL enter the cabin carrying two suitcases and a tape player. TONY is a very handsome young man in his late twenties. JILL is an attractive young woman in her early twenties. They are dressed youthfully, stylishly, quite differently from the Jacksons.)

FRANK. I mean it. Screw, screw, screw! On the sofa, in the closet, in the refrigerator, in the bathtub, on the roof, in the fireplace, in the ... *(The Jackson's are suddenly aware of the couple who are now practically standing over them. Their eyes meet.)*

TONY. *(looking down)* Hi.

FRANK. *(looking up)* Hi.

TONY. *(a beat)* How are things?

FRANK. Good. And you?

TONY. Not bad.

FRANK. That's nice. *(FRANK and PEGGY get up. They are both very embarrassed.)*

JILL. *(extends hand to PEGGY)* Hello. I'm Jill. This is Tony.

PEGGY. *(taking her hand)* Nice to meet you. We're the Jackson's. I'm Peggy and this is Frank, and if you promise not to tell our kids, we'll never do this again.

TONY. *(shaking hands)* Your secret is safe forever. *(an uneasy pause)*

FRANK. We didn't hear you pull up.

TONY. I just had my Porsche tuned up last week.

FRANK. My station wagon sounds like a truck. Everybody knows I'm coming. *(There is an awkward silence as they look at each other. Suddenly FRANK notices the couple's luggage.)* Those are suitcases.

TONY. Yes.

FRANK. Why?

TONY. Why?

FRANK. Why?

TONY. Well, we've got this place for the weekend.

FRANK. What?

PEGGY. There must be some mistake. We've got this place for the weekend.

JILL. Oh, no.

FRANK. You sure you've got the right place? The Watson Cabin?

TONY. That's right, the Watson Cabin.

PEGGY. From the Gregory Agency?

TONY. Yes.

PEGGY. From Alice Carter?

TONY. Yes.

FRANK. How do you like that. That's terrible. You sure you've got the right place? The Watson Cabin?

TONY. Yes, the Watson Cabin, right.

FRANK. Well, this is it.

JILL. I can't believe it! She rented it to another couple.

TONY. Boy, is this dumb.

FRANK. It's stupid.

PEGGY. It's awful.

JILL. Wait 'til we tell her.

FRANK. She really screwed up.

TONY. Boy, did she ever.

PEGGY. She certainly did. *(They all nod their heads. There is an awkward pause.)*

TONY. *(finally)* I'll tell you what. Let's make it fair. I'll flip you for it.

FRANK. Wait a minute!

TONY. *(takes out a coin)* It's really the only thing to do. Heads or tails?

FRANK. Hold on! We're not flipping. We're not doing anything.

TONY. No? Why not?

FRANK. Why not? Because we were here first, that's why not! Are you a lawyer?

TONY. No.

FRANK. Good, because possession is ten ninths of the law, or something like that. Besides, our things are in the bedroom already. Come on, honey, let's put away the groceries. *(FRANK takes four boxes of breakfast cereal out of the grocery bags and spreads them around the room haphazardly.)*

JILL. Gee, that really doesn't sound fair.

FRANK. Fair? If the world was fair, we wouldn't have to come up here to get away from it.

PEGGY. We're really terribly sorry about the mix-up. I guess things like this happen. We rented this cabin two months ago. Somehow it must have slipped Mrs. Carter's mind. *(PEGGY, very patiently starts gathering up the groceries that FRANK is setting about the room and putting them in the cupboard.)*

JILL. Well, that's just it. I don't know how she could have done it. We've had this cabin every year at this time for the last three years.

TONY. I even called last week to confirm it. Well, that's it. That's the last time I do business with her, that senile old bag.

FRANK. *(defensive)* Wait a minute. I met Mrs. Carter. she's my age.

TONY. Well, you know what I mean. Some people that age seem old.

FRANK. You know, I'm glad your weekend is ruined.

TONY. *(walks away upset)* I'm sorry.

PEGGY. This is really very awkward.

JILL. *(apologetically)* You have to understand. It's kind of important for us to be here. It's sort of an anniversary.

PEGGY. Sort of?

JILL. Tony and I have been living together for three years now. This is the first place we ever spent a weekend together. So you see it's very special for us.

TONY. That dope! How could she screw up like this?

JILL. We promised ourselves we'd come here every year to kind of well, reflect.

FRANK. You're not married?

JILL. No.

PEGGY. That's nice.

FRANK. What do you mean nice?

PEGGY. I had to say something.

FRANK. You came up here to reflect huh? What the hell can a couple reflect on in three years? We've been married twenty-three years. That's when you've got something to reflect on.

JILL. Twenty-three years. That's fantastic! Isn't that

fantastic, Tony? They've been married twenty-three years.

TONY. *(Still upset. Lacklustre.)* It's terrific. Hurray! Hurray!.

PEGGY. Please, no need to get hyper about it.

FRANK. Look, we're not going to tell you there weren't any rough moments. Believe me, there were. But, with all the aggravation, all the quibbling, the problems with kids, the problems with her family, especially her father, and all that garbage, we wouldn't trade it in for the world. *(puts an arm around PEGGY)* Right, Honey? *(A beat. FRANK looks at her.)*

PEGGY. Make me an offer. *(another beat)*

FRANK. *(to PEGGY)* I still hate your father.

PEGGY. I know.

FRANK. Even though he's dead, I still hate him.

PEGGY. I know. And I'm sure even though he's dead, he still hates you. *(TONY picks up a box of Cocoa Puffs that FRANK has set around the room.)*

TONY. Cocoa Puffs? Who eats Cocoa Puffs?

FRANK. *(Grabs the Cocoa Puffs from TONY.)* None of your business. *(He hands them to Peggy who puts them away. He continues taking groceries out.)*

JILL. Well, we've had our problems, too. The first year there were adjustments we had to make and some growing up to do, but we came through, didn't we, Tony?

TONY. *(still angry)* Goddamn Mrs. Carter. Old witch!

PEGGY. Just another reminder. She's Frank's age.

JILL. That's one of Tony's big hangups. It takes him longer to forgive and forget.

TONY. What do you mean, forgive and forget? We had

a standing order for this place. She knows what it means to us. How could she go and rent it out to some dumb couple!? *(catches himself)* Excuse me.

FRANK. I'm glad we beat you here.

PEGGY. It's still early. Maybe you can find another place.

TONY. Up here? On Memorial Day? Forget it. Besides, it's not so much finding another place. It's this place. This goddamn two-room, cracker box. It happens to mean something to us. Damn!

JILL. Tony, please. *(She touches his hand tenderly.)*

TONY. Ah, the hell with it. Let's get in the car and drive back to the city. I'll be outside. *(He exits.)*

PEGGY. We really are sorry.

FRANK. Yeah, tough break.

JILL. Tony gets too upset sometimes. He's used to things going his own way. He had a terrible childhood. His parents gave him everything. Look, why don't you two go on with what you were doing? Get back on the floor and pretend we never were here.

PEGGY. It's okay with me. Are you still in the mood, Frank, or will you need a couple of hours of show and tell?

FRANK. I honestly feel bad, you know that? If this vacation didn't mean so much to my wife, I'd probably give you this place.

PEGGY. You would?

FRANK. Sure. What the hell's there to do here, anyway

PEGGY. You could watch me strangle you.

JILL. That's very nice of you, but frankly, we wouldn't

take it. You were here first. You're entitled to the place.

FRANK. Yeah, but you're both kids. To kids everything is the end of the world. It probably means a lot more to you than to us, right, Peggy?

PEGGY. Whatever you say, Frank. This is your life. I'm just passing through.

JILL. You're real okay people, you know that?

FRANK. Of course.

(TONY enters carrying a bottle of champagne.)

TONY. Look, I'm, sorry I got so carried away. *(hands FRANK the bottle)* I'd like you to have this.

FRANK. Champagne?

TONY. It would just make me feel a lot better.

PEGGY. I like his style.

JILL. *(kissing TONY'S cheek)* Isn't he terrific? In spite of being spoiled rotten, he's got a good heart.

TONY. I want you to have it. We brought up several bottles. It's ice cold. I've got a small cooler in the trunk. Why don't you open it and enjoy yourselves. Have a ball and forget us.

PEGGY. Okay.

FRANK. *(examining champagne)* Hey, this is French. It's expensive stuff. We can't accept it. Besides, we're not big champagne drinkers. Mostly beer or a scotch and gingerale.

PEGGY. Frank likes anything they serve in big glasses. It's not the money. It's the principle.

FRANK. Right.

TONY. Please, take it. I acted like a real jerk and I'm ashamed of myself.

FRANK. You know, that's darn big of you to say that. It really is. I'm not so sure I could have done that ... apologized. I'm really impressed.

PEGGY. Frank had a Republican upbringing. Nobody apologizes for anything.

JILL. It's really delicious champagne. Tony doesn't like it that much, but he buys it for me. I love it. *(Kisses TONY'S ear and straightens his hair.)* ... and I love him, too. You fabulous, great-looking person.

TONY. *(to JILL)* I'm wild about you, you know that.

JILL. I know that.

FRANK. *(looks on fondly; to PEGGY)* Bring back memories?

PEGGY. Not really ... *(TONY picks up a box of Captain Crunch that FRANK has just put out.)*

TONY. Captain Crunch! You eat this crap too?

FRANK. *(pulling it away from him)* Give me that! *(He hands it to PEGGY who puts it in the cupboard. FRANK continues to take out the groceries but at a much slower pace.)*

JILL. I was awful lucky to get a guy like Tony. I remember the first time I saw him. I was at a party and having a terrible time. I was with this dentist. Then Tony walked in and I just knew he was the guy for me. I went home with him that night, and we've been together ever since.

FRANK. What happened to the dentist?

JILL. He's fine. In fact we both go to him.

FRANK. That's terrific. Now that's what I call a love story. Why can't they make movies about nice situations like that instead of all those dumb sex movies. Boy, do I hate them. That's why I stopped taking Peg to the movies years ago.

PEGGY. Frank's a real prude. He even found Cinderella disgusting.

TONY. That's too bad. *(tugs at JILL'S arm)* Come on. We'd better get going. *(to FRANK and PEGGY)* Look, I hope you two have a great weekend. Enjoy the champagne.

JILL. Yes. Well, nice meeting you both.

PEGGY. Bye.

FRANK. Wait a minute! I'll tell you what. We'll accept your champagne on one condition.

PEGGY. *(concerned)* What condition, Frank?

FRANK. That they stay and have dinner with us. I mean, damn it, they just drove all the way from the city, what kind of a guy would send them right back?

PEGGY. *(fearful)* Not a guy like you.

FRANK. Uh uh.

TONY. Please, that's not necessary. Actually, I wasn't planning to go right back to the city. There's a little town about thirty miles from here. I was going to check to see if they might have something.

FRANK. You can go if you want, but then we won't accept the champagne.

JILL. That's silly.

PEGGY. Isn't it?

FRANK. I mean it. I won't take the champagne.

PEGGY. Frank, maybe they prefer being alone. Like some other people we know in this room.

FRANK. Don't be ridiculous. They've been together a long time. It's not like a first date. Besides, we're going to be up here three days. At least we'll have someone to talk to for awhile. *(to TONY and JILL)* Now, what do you say?

TONY. Well, we really couldn't.

JILL. It's just too much of an imposition.

FRANK. It's not at all. I really want you to stay. It would make me feel a lot better about you getting screwed out of the cabin. We've got tons of food. Ham, roast beef, chicken, you name it. One thing I always insist on is that there's plenty of food, right, Peg?

PEGGY. When Frank was a kid his mother told him if he ever missed a meal, he would get Leprosy.

FRANK. Peggy will make fried chicken and that's that.

PEGGY. She will?

TONY. Oh, no, if we stay, we can't have you cooking for us.

FRANK. Why not?

PEGGY. *(to TONY)* Why not?

TONY. Because this is supposed to be a vacation.

PEGGY. *(to FRANK)* He's got a point.

FRANK. So what? Peggy has to cook anyway. It's just as easy to cook for four as it is for two.

PEGGY. *(innocently)* No kidding. I didn't know that.

FRANK. Oh, sure. What is it to make fried chicken anyway? Some oil, some bread crumbs, a chicken and a plate for the bones.

PEGGY. What a recipe. How can I miss.

JILL. Absolutely not. It's terrible to have to cook on a vacation.

FRANK. Believe me, she doesn't mind. We've got three

kids. She's used to it. Right, Peg?

PEGGY. It's statements like that, Frank, that make me wish I knew karate.

JILL. Look, I have the perfect solution. We have a bunch of frozen dinners on dry ice.

FRANK. Frozen dinners? Get off it. My wife wouldn't let me eat one of those in a million years. Right, Peg?

PEGGY. Wrong, Frank.

FRANK. You would?

PEGGY. And I'm not so sure I'd defrost it first, either.

TONY. They're really super. It's not your run of the mill frozen food. There's this one restaurant, La Maison. You've heard of it?

FRANK. Of course, I've heard of it and I wouldn't go there. It's way over-priced. You end up paying strictly for atmosphere.

PEGGY. Atmosphere to Frank is anything more than a paper napkin.

TONY. Well, they prepare these frozen dinners that are unbelievable. They have duck and veal and lobster, fancy sauces, fancy vegetables, the works. They're fabulous.

PEGGY. My vote is yes and I'll take the lobster.

FRANK. I don't know. Frozen food, you get such small portions.

JILL. You can have two. We've got a dozen of them. They cost eighteen dollars each and we'd just end up throwing them away.

FRANK. Eighteen dollars for a frozen dinner? Are you a rich kid?

TONY. Well, I do alright.

JILL. Tony works for his father.

FRANK. What does your father do?

TONY. Real estate.

FRANK. Selling it?

TONY. Buying it. Anyone can sell it.

PEGGY. Frank's in office supplies.

FRANK. J and D Office Supplies. Wholesale Only. The J is me, Jackson, and the D is for my partner, Harvey Daniels. Not a bad guy. He's made a few mistakes but we've done okay. You ought to see the paper they're using for next year's calendars. Real crap. I net fifty thousand a year. Not bad, huh?

TONY. No. That's very nice.

FRANK. I think so. What about you? What kind of money do you knock down?

PEGGY. Frank, that's rude.

FRANK. No, he wants to tell me, let him tell me.

TONY. I guess I make around sixty-five thousand a year.

FRANK. *(disappointed)* You do?

FRANK. Well, actually I net about seventy. I didn't want to brag. *(to JILL)* How about you? I'll bet you're a model, or something.

JILL. Yes, how did you know?

FRANK. It figures. You're built like a brick shithouse. Remember when you had a figure like that, Peg?

PEGGY. Thank you, Frank.

JILL. Look, it's yes on the frozen food, right?

PEGGY. Right.

TONY. Right.

FRANK. Okay, okay. I give up. Majority rules.

PEGGY. What a prince.

FRANK. I never denied it.

TONY. I'll get the food.

JILL. And the candles. We brought candles. I love to eat by candlelight, don't you?

PEGGY. We haven't done that for years.

JILL. Why not? It's so romantic.

FRANK. Maybe, but I like to see what I'm eating.

TONY. Come on, Frank. You can give me a hand.

FRANK. Sure. *(On his way toward the door, TONY picks up the box of Sugar Bangs.)*

TONY. Sugar Bangs?

FRANK. It's new. Somebody's got to try it. *(FRANK takes the cereal and puts it on the counter.)*

JILL. *(crossing to TONY)* You'd better bring in a few more bottles of champagne, too. Let's make this a night to remember.

TONY. Okay, with me. *(They kiss. FRANK looks at them admiringly.)*

PEGGY. A night to remember. There was a movie once with that title. As I recall ... *(suddenly concerned)* ... it was about the sinking of the Titanic. *(In unison, the three look at PEGGY.)*

BLACKOUT

Scene Two

Time: Saturday morning.

FRANK and PEGGY are dressed in appropriate casual clothes. PEGGY is folding the sheets on the open sofa bed. FRANK is pacing.

FRANK. I can't believe it. Nine o'clock in the morning, and they're still sleeping.

PEGGY. Young people like to sleep late.

FRANK. What for? They're on vacation. They should get up and do things. You can sleep late any time.

PEGGY. Look, why don't you just knock on the door and tell them you have to go to the bathroom.

FRANK. I can't. It's too embarrassing.

PEGGY. Then go outside in the bushes some place.

FRANK. I can't. I have to make a big one.

PEGGY. You want me to knock on the door?

FRANK. No, I'll just wait.

PEGGY. You've got real hang-ups, you know that, Frank?

FRANK. I can't help it. It's a problem. I hate people knowing when I'm going to the bathroom. You just don't know how I suffered in the Army. Six johns in one room. No stalls, Everything was open. It was embarrassing. I only went twice a week and at three o'clock in the morning.

25

PEGGY. Look, you invited them, not me.

FRANK. What could I do? We couldn't send them out so late at night with no place to go.

PEGGY. But to invite them for the whole weekend?

FRANK. I did? Not the whole weekend? That damn champagne! I'm not used to that stuff. It makes me too friendly.

PEGGY. And to give them the bedroom. They could have slept out here. But you insisted.

FRANK. I wanted to be near the refrigerator. Sometimes when I can't sleep, I like to get up and stare at the fruit.

PEGGY. That's very weird, Frank.

FRANK. I know. That's why I never told you before ... You know what else? I've got a headache. That champagne couldn't have been too good.

PEGGY. Frank, you drank two and a half bottles. You can get a headache from Seven Up if you drink two and a half bottles.

FRANK. Well, I'm through with the French and all their wine. Those people enjoy getting Americans sick. You know I don't even remember eating dinner. What the hell was it I had anyway?

PEGGY. Lobster Newburg. Beef Strogonoff and Veal Cordon Bleu.

FRANK. I ate all that?

PEGGY. I'm afraid so.

FRANK. Did I like it?

PEGGY. You loved it.

FRANK. What about the duck? I really wanted the duck.

PEGGY. Don't ask about the duck.

FRANK. No?

PEGGY. No.

FRANK. Why am I still alive?

PEGGY. It's got me stumped.

FRANK. Jesus Christ, are they going to stay in bed all day? Next time we rent a cabin, I'm making sure the bathroom is in the living room where I can get to it. *(goes to the door and gives a rooster crow)*

PEGGY. Frank, that was very dumb. There are no chickens in these woods.

FRANK. I'm desperate.

PEGGY. Why don't you just open the door quietly and go into the bathroom?

FRANK. I can't do that. Remember, they're not married. They're probably sleeping naked.

PEGGY. Maybe you'd like to have breakfast now. It might get your mind off of things.

FRANK. It won't. I have to keep moving.

PEGGY. Well, the coffee's ready and I'm going to have a cup.

FRANK. Do what you want. Just don't tell me about it.

PEGGY. Maybe if you tried talking about something.

FRANK. Like what?

PEGGY. Anything. Pick a subject.

FRANK. Going home.

PEGGY. Try again.

FRANK. Staying home.

PEGGY. Why don't we gossip. That's always fun.

FRANK. All right. What do we talk about?

PEGGY. *(indicates bedroom)* How about them? *(She pours herself a cup of coffee.)*

FRANK. He'll never marry her.

PEGGY. That was quick.

FRANK. And she's lucky. I think he's a smart ass.

PEGGY. I think he's very patient. He sat there for hours listening to you talk about office supplies.

FRANK. I happen to make the subject very interesting.

PEGGY. Robert Redford couldn't make the subject interesting.

FRANK. If I was that boring, why did he accept my invitation for the rest of the weekend? I'll tell you why. He stayed because he respects me. He admires a selfmade man. I didn't get the world handed to me on a silver platter like he did and it impressed the hell out of him.

PEGGY. That's not why he stayed, Frank.

FRANK. Then give me a better reason.

PEGGY. You hid his car keys.

FRANK. *(nods)* God, I wonder where I put them.

PEGGY. I found them in the coffee pot. *(She picks keys up off the counter to show FRANK.)*

FRANK. What a relief. Maybe they'll go now. You know all they want out of life is a good time.

PEGGY. What's wrong with that?

FRANK. It isn't good for the country. Everybody starts enjoying themselves, they let their guard down and before you know it Jimmy Carter's our president again. And another thing that griped me. I thought the discussion about sex was unnecessary. I got a little mad when he asked me if it was still as much fun at our age.

PEGGY. Well, I got a little annoyed with your answer.

FRANK. Why? What did I say?

PEGGY. No.

FRANK. I did?

PEGGY. You did.

FRANK. I was just being honest. We've been married a long time. There are interruptions, kids, pets, phone calls ... How can it be fun?

PEGGY. Shut up, Frank.

FRANK. Well, it was none of his business anyway. Sex is a very private thing. I don't even like telling you about it ... And the two of them, all that kissing and hugging ... that's not love.

PEGGY. No?

FRANK. No. That's passion.

PEGGY. I'll take it.

FRANK. Grow up, Peggy. Passion comes and goes but love is like a rock.

PEGGY. Did you just make that up?

FRANK. *(proudly)* Yes.

PEGGY. It stinks.

FRANK. Let me explain it very simply. When we were young, we had plenty of hot times, didn't we?

PEGGY. I guess so.

FRANK. Believe me, that was passion. What we've got now is love. So there it is.

PEGGY. I don't get it.

FRANK. Me neither. It's the damn champagne. *(goes to door and puts his ear against it)* Are they going to stay in bed all day long? *(crows like a rooster again and then leaves)* You know what really upsets me about them?

PEGGY. I haven't a clue.

FRANK. They've got it too damn easy. They've been everywhere, Spain, Italy, ... skiing in Switzerland.

PEGGY. Great life, huh?

FRANK. Hell no! If you go everywhere now, what have you got left when you get old?

PEGGY. Memories. Memories of beautiful, unusual places, of romance and adventure.

FRANK. And what about the flies and the bad food and the poor service?

PEGGY. Frank, there's plenty of that in this country.

FRANK. That's the point I'm making. Why travel for it?

PEGGY. Are you trying to drive me crazy?

(The door opens and TONY and JILL come out.)

TONY. Hi.

JILL. Good morning.

FRANK. Good morning. *(He rushes past them and into the bedroom.)*

PEGGY. Did you sleep okay?

TONY. Great.

JILL. It was wonderful. I didn't open my eyes till I heard the the rooster. Is that coffee I smell?

PEGGY. Yes. Like some?

JILL. Love some.

TONY. Make it two.

PEGGY. We haven't had our breakfast yet. Bacon and eggs all right with you?

TONY. No, just coffee, thanks.

PEGGY. That's it?

JILL. That's all we ever have for breakfast.

PEGGY. Me, too, but if Frank doesn't have his bacon and eggs every morning, he stays totally irrational.

JILL. What about all that sweet cereal?

PEGGY. I won't let him eat any till after twelve. I can tolerate the crunching when he eats it plain but when he adds milk, the slurping is deafening.

TONY. You know, we really enjoyed ourselves last night.

PEGGY. I'm glad. We did, too. *(PEGGY pours coffee for them and then begins preparing FRANK's breakfast.)*

JILL. It was really nice of you and Frank to invite us to stay. It means so much to us to be here this weekend.

TONY. At first I wasn't so sure it was going to work out, but after Frank stopped talking about stationery, it started going pretty well.

JILL. He's really a sweet person.

PEGGY. Frank is very sweet.

JILL. Once he lets himself go, he's really something. I think his tap dancing on the table was hilarious.

PEGGY. It was, wasn't it?

TONY. Especially after he stepped in the duck. I thought I'd die watching him try to get it off his foot.

PEGGY. Yes, too bad he couldn't wait until we finished dinner.

JILL. He really has a terrific sense of humor. I think a sense of humor is very important in a man.

(FRANK comes out of the bathroom. He is sullen.)

FRANK. I waited too damn long. I'm constipated. *(toTONY)* Listen, for tomorrow, we're going to have to work out a system on the bathroom.

TONY. Gee, I'm sorry. Why didn't you knock, or come right in?

FRANK. I didn't want to wake you.

PEGGY. It wouldn't have mattered. The rooster woke them.

FRANK. *(to TONY and JILL)* I want to ask you two something. You've been here before. It's a nice place, it's pretty, but what the hell do you do all day long?

JILL. Well, the first time it was kind of a honeymoon.

FRANK. Okay, that's one year. But after that, what?

TONY. Well, we don't really do much of anything. We kind of just hang around with each other, you know, talk to each other, listen to music, hold hands...

FRANK. *(to PEGGY)* See, I told you. There's nothing to do here.

TONY. A lot of times we just go for walks. There's a terrific little lake about a mile down the hill.

FRANK. So?

TONY. So, we go down there.

FRANK. And?

TONY. And we throw stones in the water.

FRANK. And?

TONY. And that's it.

FRANK. That's it?

TONY. That's it.

JILL. It's great just being together with nothing to do, nothing to worry about.

PEGGY. To Frank a day without worry is a day without sunshine.

FRANK. That's not so. I just like to keep my mind active. You know what they say? Use it or lose it.

PEGGY. Bad news, Frank. They weren't talking about your mind.

TONY. Hey, why don't we all take a walk down to the lake right now?

FRANK. I can't. I haven't had my breakfast.

JILL. We'll wait until after you eat.

FRANK. I don't think so. I read you should never exercise on a full stomach. Is there a road? Maybe we can drive.

PEGGY. That's not very romantic.

FRANK. It's nine o'clock. You know as well as I do romance doesn't start 'til the sun goes down.

JILL. That's ridiculous.

PEGGY. No, that's Frank.

TONY. Frank, you actually put love on a schedule?

FRANK. Did I say that? I never said that. We weren't talking about love. We were talking about romance. You know, perfume and flowers and moonlight and violins and all that crap. That's romance. The love part, Peggy and I already discussed and if you're really interested, she'll fill you in while I'm having my breakfast.

PEGGY. Frank, I think you're presenting these two kids with a very dismal picture of marital bliss.

FRANK. I love marriage, but they might as well get used to the idea that when a couple has been together a long time, the romance part goes without saying.

JILL. You mean you take each other for granted?

FRANK. Of course. That's the beauty of it. There's no pressure. I love her. She loves me. She knows it. I know it. And we don't have to hold hands all morning and throw stones in the water to prove it. Right, Peg?

PEGGY. For the first time in my life, Frank, I'm going to burn your eggs.

JILL. Maybe I'm naive, but to me the worst thing a couple can do is to take each other for granted. A relationship should be filled with surprises, excitement.

TONY. Once it becomes routine, it's in trouble.

FRANK. *(to PEGGY)* Obviously, these two can't see what you and I have.

PEGGY. I'm dying to hear the list.

FRANK. *(puts his arm around her)* We have contentment. We have security. We have trust. Our marriage is like time. It's endless.

PEGGY. I think you mean eternal.

FRANK. Maybe I do, maybe I don't. Anyway, I didn't come up here to talk about marriage.

JILL. I'm sorry. I didn't mean to upset you, but you see by examining other relationships, well, it sort of helps us define ours.

PEGGY. What's wrong with your relationship? You seem very happy.

JILL. We are. But we like to see why other people sometimes ... aren't.

FRANK. What are you talking about? You think we're not? *(PEGGY places FRANK's eggs on the table. He sits and begins eating.)*

JILL. No. Of course not. I mean, I wasn't talking about you specifically, I was talking about other people, generally.

FRANK. Other people? What other people? We're the only ones here.

JILL. Frank, I think we're having a problem communicating.

FRANK. To hell with communicating. Let me set you straight right now. You're looking at a happy man. *(indicates smile on his face)* See! Ha Ha! By the way ... *(Holds up car keys.)* Here are your car keys in case you want to go anywhere.

TONY. Thanks.

JILL. Do you want to know why we're so happy ... Tony and I?

FRANK. No.! *(JILL sits on TONY'S lap and puts her arms around his neck.)*

JILL. Because we love to touch one another. Even when we're sleeping. It's important to us. Do you still touch Peggy a lot, Frank?

FRANK. If you two are looking to have an orgy, you've got the wrong couple.

TONY. You see, we feel that there's no reason why a couple in their twenties can't love each other the same way when they're in their fifties.

PEGGY. Well, that's where Frank has you. He's always loved me like he was fifty.

FRANK. Wait a minute. Why the hell is everyone picking on me?

PEGGY. You happen to be very easy, Frank. Maybe that's your charm.

JILL. We're not trying to pick on you, Frank. It's just that that's the way the conversation drifted.

FRANK. Yeah? Well, let it drift the hell out of here. I'm through talking. You got that, kids?

JILL. I apologize.

FRANK. Too late.

JILL. Come on, Tony. I think we'd better go for a walk.

TONY. You sure you don't want to go, Frank?

PEGGY. Come on, Frank. It might do us some good.

FRANK. If the four of us go for a walk together all we'll do is talk and I'll get in more trouble. No, Peggy and I will stay right here. Maybe I'll get undressed, get back in bed, get up, get dressed again and try to start the morning all over.

JILL. Oh, come one, Frank. it's good exercise.

FRANK. I don't need to exercise.

TONY. You should. You'll feel better.

FRANK. I feel fine.

TONY. A lot of guys your age even jog.

FRANK. Will you lay off the age thing! Look, I happen to be in pretty damn good shape. I went for a checkup a few years ago, and there was hardly anything wrong with me.

TONY. It's your body.

FRANK. You don't believe me, do you?

TONY. Well, Frank, it stands to reason if you don't exercise and you don't do anything physical, you couldn't be in great shape.

FRANK. Okay, I'll tell you what. (Stands and takes out a bill.) Here's five dollars, I'll race you for it.

PEGGY. Frank, come on.

TONY. Don't be silly, Frank.

FRANK. A hundred-yard dash. Five bucks. You want to make it ten, we'll make it ten. *(pulls out another bill)*

PEGGY. Frank, you're being childish.

FRANK. I was one of the fastest kids on the block.

PEGGY. That was years ago. Your legs are much older now.

FRANK. I don't need the legs. I've got the heart.

PEGGY. That's another thing to consider. The heart is much older, too.

FRANK. B.S. I'm in as good shape as any man ten years younger than me.

PEGGY. So that still makes you forty-three. Tony is in his twenties.

FRANK. *(to TONY)* Ten bucks. A hundred-yard dash. Have we got a deal, or not?

TONY. I don't think it's a good idea.

FRANK. It's a great idea. I'm challenging you. *(pointing out the window)* See that tree over there? From that tree to where the road turns off. Ten bucks.

TONY. All right, you've got it.

FRANK. Now you're talking. *(He puts his ten dollars on the table.)* Come on, everyone. I need a rooting section.

TONY. *(puts ten dollars on the table)* Here's my ten.

PEGGY. I'm not going to watch.

JILL. Me neither.

TONY. *(Takes off his shirt and hands it to JILL.)* Here, hold this.

FRANK. *(Takes off his sweater and hands it to PEGGY. He has a shirt underneath.)* Here! You hold this.

PEGGY. Frank, be careful. You're not as young as you...

FRANK. *(Anticipating her next word.)* I am too! *(to TONY)* Come on. Let's go.

TONY. *(opening door for FRANK)* After you. *(They exit.)*

JILL. This is dumb!

PEGGY. He's really impossible today.

JILL. Is he mad at Tony? I hope not.

PEGGY. No. I just think it's a simple case of an adding machine wishing like hell that the computer wasn't invented.

FRANK. *(off stage)* Get on your mark!

PEGGY. I refuse to look at this.

JILL. Me, too.

FRANK. *(off stage)* Get set!

PEGGY. It's ridiculous!

JILL. It really is.

FRANK. *(off stage)* Go! *(PEGGY and JILL rush to the window.)*

PEGGY. Come on, Frank!

JILL. Look at him go, for his age!

PEGGY. Faster, Frank! Faster!

JILL. He's just a few yards behind.

PEGGY. *(yelling)* Watch out for that tree, Frank!

(We hear a painful scream. It's FRANK.)

JILL. He hit the tree!

PEGGY. I don't believe it!

JILL. I think he's all right. Tony's picking him up.

PEGGY. How could he run into a tree? *(She leaves the window, a bit disappointed.)*

JILL. *(still observing)* Oh, no!

PEGGY. What's wrong? Now?

JILL. He tricked him! He tricked Tony!

PEGGY. *(rushing to the window)* What?

JILL. When Tony came to help him, Frank pushed him over and ran to the finish line.

PEGGY. I don't believe it. I'd expect that from someone in the oil business but not in office supplies.

JILL. It was the funniest thing I ever saw. Boy, did Tony get his.

PEGGY. *(at the door)* Frank, you should be ashamed of yourself.

(FRANK enters.)

FRANK. Did I show him? Did I show the kid? You don't mess with Frank Jackson.

PEGGY. That was unfair and ... well, just a terrible thing to do. *(Picks up the money and hands it to FRANK.)* Here, the money is yours.

FRANK. Thanks.

(TONY enters.)

FRANK. *(He extends his hand.)* Nice race.

TONY. You cheated.

FRANK. Of course. How else could I win?

TONY. Next time we go over the rules first.

FRANK. Forget it. Rules are for amateurs. Pros go right for the jugular.

PEGGY. Very philosophical.

PEGGY. The facts of life! Maybe later I'll let him win his money back.

TONY. I have a feeling I won't.

FRANK. You're probably right.

JILL. *(fixing TONY'S hair)* Look at your hair. It's a mess.

TONY. Frank turned out to be a tiger after all.

FRANK. You bet your ass.

JILL. You know, that's the first time I saw you lose at anything.

TONY. Are you disappointed?

JILL. No, just a little surprised.

TONY. Come on now. Let's go for that walk.

JILL. *(to FRANK and PEGGY)* You two sure you don't want to come with us?

FRANK. Maybe next time. Now that I'm in the mood, I may want to do three hundred sit-ups.

JILL. Well, we'll see you.

TONY. *(extending his hand to FRANK)* You ran a crooked race, Frank.

FRANK. Thanks. *(He shakes TONY'S hand.)*

PEGGY. We'll have lunch around one.

TONY. Great. Bye!

PEGGY. Bye. *(TONY and JILL exit.)*

FRANK. *(When he's sure they're gone he collapses to the sofa.)* Ahhhhhh!

PEGGY. Frank, are okay?

FRANK. Is my face purple? My face feels purple.

PEGGY. You look fine.

FRANK. Are you proud of me?

PEGGY. Yes and no.

FRANK. I like the yes part the best.

PEGGY. You shouldn't have cheated.

FRANK. Does it matter?

PEGGY. For some strange reason, it doesn't. *(She sits down beside him.)*

FRANK. You know what I think they think ... I think they think *(He puts his arm around PEGGY.)* we're two old farts.

PEGGY. I know. Its awful, isn't it?

FRANK. I guess so. But it is sort of a cozy feeling, isn't it? *(They snuggle happily.)*

DIM OUT

Scene Three

Time: Saturday night. A current rock and roll tape is playing.

> *TONY is on the floor reading a book. JILL has her head on his lap. PEGGY is doing stitchery. FRANK is pacing around. Obviously the music annoys him. He glares at TONY and JILL and then finally goes to the tape player and shuts it off. To his surprise, no one says anything.*

TONY. *(looking up)* You've got to go to Europe, Frank.

FRANK. Why?

TONY. I'm reading this book that takes place in Paris

and it just reminded me how fantastic it is. *(He goes back to his book.)*

PEGGY. *(a beat)* I'd love to go to Europe.

FRANK. What for? They hate us there.

PEGGY. I just thought I'd like to see it someday.

FRANK. Too damn expensive.

JILL. Depends on how you go.

FRANK. How did you go?

TONY. Well, we went the expensive way. But there are other ways.

FRANK. Who needs it?

JILL. I loved Paris, but my favorite place of all was Mazatlan.

FRANK. Where the hell's that?

TONY. Mexico.

FRANK. What did you go there for?

TONY. Just to go.

FRANK. I'll bet you got sick.

JILL. No.

FRANK. Most people get sick.

JILL. Tony and I are lucky. We never get sick when we travel.

FRANK. Too bad. It might be good for you once in awhile.

JILL. God, the beaches were pure white, weren't they, Tony? And the water was crystal blue and the air, it was just unbelievable.

PEGGY. Oh, I'd love to go there.

FRANK. Too dangerous.

PEGGY. What do you mean too dangerous? It sounds wonderful.

FRANK. That's my point. We're city people. Our bodies wouldn't function in a wonderful environment.

JILL. You know what was the biggest disappointment? Sri Lanka. It's gotten so commercial.

FRANK. Can I give you two a little tip about travel?

PEGGY. Here it comes again, gang.

FRANK. It's all hype. If those places were so great, they wouldn't have to advertise. You want to have a great time? Check into a good hotel in town. You don't have to worry about the airlines losing your luggage and you don't have to deal with foreigners cursing you in weird languages.

PEGGY. Anybody else want to share a little philosophy?

TONY. Everyone travels now, Frank. It's no big deal.

FRANK. I travel enough. We're going to Cincinnati in March.

PEGGY. I didn't know that.

FRANK. Well, it's not definite yet. I was saving it as a surprise. Hallmark is showing their new line.

PEGGY. Cincinnati in March. I hope I can take the culture shock.

FRANK. There's nothing wrong with Cincinnati. I heard they're fixing it up. *(He goes to the cupboard takes out the box of Cocoa Puffs and begins eating them like popcorn.)*

TONY. I think you and Peggy should go to Europe, Frank.

FRANK. What the hell for? We've got everything they've got and it's not as old.

TONY. Just to get a new perspective on things. It doesn't hurt to know what's going on in the rest of the world.

FRANK. I know what's going on in the rest of the world, and I'm sick about it. I don't have to go see it. I don't understand kids today, running, running, running. What the hell for?

TONY. To see it while we're here. To be on our own. To be independent, to learn new things, to broaden our outlook.

FRANK. If you're going to be vague, let's just drop it.

JILL. God, Frank, what was your youth like? You came from the generation of hippies and peace demonstrators and love-ins...

PEGGY. Frank was born wearing a tie. Need I say more?

FRANK. Responsibility!

TONY. What about it?

FRANK. I was born with that, too. Not everyone had time to sing songs and carry posters. I was getting a family started and that's where my priorities were. Okay, I haven't been to a lot of places or done a lot of things but that doesn't mean I don't know what's going on. I mean, I read the paper, I watch the news. I know more about this world than most people and I know what's important in life and what's not.

PEGGY. What is important, Frank?

FRANK. There are a lot of important things.

JILL. Health.

FRANK. That's right. Health. That's one of them.

JILL. Most older people choose that one first.

FRANK. What do you mean older? You think we're old?

PEGGY. She means older than her and Tony.

JILL. Right.

FRANK. Let me teach you kids something right now. Twenties, thirties, fifties, eighties ... Age is meaningless. It's in the head. Right now if you were to ask me how old I was, I'd have to stop and think about it.

PEGGY. That's because you're older. Your thinking process has slowed down.

FRANK. Let me tell you something about being my age, fifty-one.

PEGGY. Fifty-three!

FRANK. Whatever. It's wonderful. You know why it's wonderful? Because at my age, the clouds have parted and you start to understand it all, every bit of it.

TONY. Every bit of what?

FRANK. Every bit of what life is. Of what we were talking about. Of what's important.

JILL. Well, we know health was number one. What's two?

FRANK. I'm getting a headache, folks.

PEGGY. That comes under health.

FRANK. There are a lot of things that are important. A good job, a good wife, good friends, good neighbors, a good auto mechanic...

TONY. I call you on the auto mechanic.

FRANK. To me that's important. I put thirty thousand miles a year on my car.

TONY. *(sighs)* You know what I find wrong with you?

FRANK. If you value your life, you won't tell me.

PEGGY. Don't be a wet blanket, Frank. I have my own ideas, but I'd like to hear a second opinion.

TONY. Your whole existence is right on the nose. Everything about you is black and white. There's no room for imagination, thought, intellectual growth.

FRANK. Did you go to college?

TONY. Yes.

FRANK. That was your first mistake.

TONY. You're a man without poetry, without dreams, without vision. It's an empty way to live. It's stupid, it's wasteful, it's pathetic.

FRANK. Do you believe this guy? Here's a guy who drives a Porsche, drinks champagne, lives off his old man, and he's telling me I'm pathetic. Okay, wise guy. You want to know what's really important to me? Do you?

JILL. Way to go, Frank. Take another shot at it.

PEGGY. I'd think it over first, Frank.

FRANK. Inner peace.

JILL. I like it! It's a very Zen beginning.

FRANK. Inner peace is important to me, and that's what I have and you two don't. The feeling that everything is all right. That nothing that happens is life or death.

PEGGY. I would quit now, Frank.

FRANK. No anxieties, no fears. Me, coming to terms with myself after years of struggling, of trials and tribulations, of ups and downs ... To finally accept what's become of me and not blame anybody. To be what I am, a satisfied man. A man totally fulfilled and content to spend the rest of my life watching the passing parade. *(Puts his arm around PEGGY.)* And Peggy, I want you to know you're a very big part of this contentment. You helped find it, you helped make it and thanks loads.

PEGGY. I don't know why, but suddenly I'm depressed.

TONY. Is that it?

FRANK. That's it.

TONY. Frank, it's obvious to me, your life is shit.

FRANK. *(calmly)* Shit? ... *(looks at PEGGY)* Shit? ... *(angry)* Shit! *(He goes to TONY and throws a headlock on him.)*

TONY. Hey!

PEGGY. Frank!

FRANK. You want to know what's important? Right now this is important. That I hurt you. *(PEGGY and JILL try to free TONY.)*

JILL. He's killing him!

FRANK. Right!

TONY. *(being strangled)* This is healthy, Frank. This is exactly the way I acted the first day with my shrink when he said things I didn't want to hear.

FRANK. *(tightening his grip)* A shrink! You think I need a shrink?

TONY. I think most people can use some help. I believe in getting help. Help!

PEGGY. Let him go, Frank.

FRANK. I'm getting him, then I'm getting her, then I'm going home and getting our kids. *(The girls finally free TONY from FRANK'S grip. TONY jumps to his feet.)*

TONY. *(rubbing his neck)* Boy, Frank, having a meaningful conversation with you is murder.

JILL. Tony was just trying to help.

FRANK. Help what?

TONY. Help the two of you understand your lives better. It's obvious you're having problems.

FRANK. We're having problems? *(points toward bed-room)* Bedtime!

PEGGY. Frank...

FRANK. *(picking up log from fireplace)* Bedtime or I part your hair with this log.

TONY. *(sighs)* Come on, honey. It's getting late anyway.

JILL. *(sincerely)* It was really another terrific day.

FRANK. Speak for yourself.

TONY. *(fatherly)* Look, Frank, later on if you change your mind ... if you want to talk about things ... anything ... we're good listeners.

FRANK. *(sharply)* Good night!

JILL. Good night.

TONY. *(at the bedroom door)* And if you have to use the bathroom, just come in and use it. If there's anything happening, we'll lock the door for a few hours. *(They exit.)*

FRANK. *(a beat)* A few hours?

PEGGY. It was fun being young, remember?

FRANK. You know what I wish for them? When they walk out of that room tomorrow they're ten years older than us. Boy, could we give it to them!

PEGGY. Is that what's bothering you, Frank? That we've gotten older?

FRANK. I don't know. Yes ... No ... Maybe ... I don't know. *(PEGGY prepares their bed. FRANK starts to un-dress.)*

PEGGY. You know, Tony was right. You're on the nose, Frank. I can tell what time of day it is by what you're doing, by your every mood.

FRANK. I'm just set in my ways. That's not so bad. That's stability. A lot of women wish their husbands had that.

PEGGY. And it's not just you. It's me, too. We never really do anything new or different.

FRANK. Look, I tried smoking pot, remember? But I couldn't inhale.

PEGGY. We lack something, Frank. We lack style.

FRANK. Don't give me that.

PEGGY. We just don't have it. I don't care how much money I spend on clothes, I still look like somebody's mother.

FRANK. You are.

PEGGY. I wish I was brave enough to do something really ... drastic.

FRANK. Like what?

PEGGY. I don't know. Maybe ... Maybe change the color of my hair ... or have a face lift.

FRANK. That's style?

PEGGY. I don't know. But at least it's a departure. I just don't think the things I do make it. Even the furniture I pick out. I don't buy cheap furniture, Frank, but when I get it in the house, it's just wrong.

FRANK. You had an interior decorator.

PEGGY. Even my interior decorator was wrong.

FRANK. I told you to use a fag.

PEGGY. I thought he was. I was wrong there, too.

FRANK. Look, I like you the way you are, but if you want to change your hair and your face, do it.

PEGGY. Something is missing in us, Frank. Being

around those two young kids makes me feel it even more.

FRANK. *(suddenly becoming very serious, very tender)* You really want to know how those two make me feel? I'll tell you. I feel like they're pushing us right off this earth. And they are. Every second that goes by someone like Tony and Jill are right behind us gobbling up our time ... our moments that we're not quite finished with. And damn it, they seem to be making more out of them than us. Mexico! Paris! Charge it! Have fun! Go places! Live together! ... I could never let myself do that. *(a beat)* I once used to laugh at my father. He always took his lunch to work in a brown paper bag and he always brought the empty bag home to use again. I laughed at him because that was the one thing he really didn't have to do. He could have had all the bags he wanted. He worked for a grocery store. For some stupid reason I feel like my father now. I feel like I'm being laughed at.

PEGGY. I'm not laughing at you, Frank. I'm really not.

FRANK. No ... No, you're not. *(sighs)* They're pushing us out, Peggy. They're making us feel obsolete. God-damn it, I hate young people. I said it and I'm glad. I hate them! I hate them! *(He gets on the sofa and starts jumping up and down.)* I hate young people! I hate young people! I hate young people!

(The bedroom door opens and TONY and JILL come out and look at FRANK in bewilderment.)

TONY. Anything wrong?

FRANK. Kids!

TONY. Yes?

FRANK. This is for you! *(He turns around, lowers his pants and moons at them.)*

PEGGY. *(screaming)* Frank!

FAST CURTAIN

END OF ACT ONE

ACT TWO

Scene One

Time: Sunday morning.

It is almost the identical scene as in Act One Scene Two. FRANK and PEGGY are dressed in appropriate clothing. PEGGY is folding the sheets on the open sofa bed. FRANK is pacing.

FRANK. *(finally)* He knows I have to go to the bathroom. I know he knows.

PEGGY. I'm sure they just forgot to unlock the door. Why don't you knock?

FRANK. I'm not going to give him the satisfaction.

PEGGY. What satisfation?

FRANK. He wants me to think he's having sex in there. I want him to know that I couldn't care less and besides I don't have to go to the bathroom any more because I think I'm constipated again and here comes another miserable day.

PEGGY. *(a beat)* That's too bad.

FRANK. You still mad at me?

PEGGY. No.

FRANK. Yes, you are.

PEGGY. Well, what you did wasn't very nice.

FRANK. I enjoyed it. I finally got things off my mind.

PEGGY. They didn't think it was funny.

FRANK. They're too sensitive. That's why young people don't make good politicians.

PEGGY. It wasn't just dropping your pants that got them mad. It was when you stood at attention stark naked and sang the National Anthem that I thought you touched on bad taste.

FRANK. You know, I really surprised myself. I didn't think I knew all the words.

PEGGY. Well, it just wasn't like you.

FRANK. I know.

PEGGY. *(starting to laugh)* It was funny as hell, though.

FRANK. *(smiling)* Yeah, I thought so, too.

PEGGY. *(indicating bedroom)* They were up all night long talking.

FRANK. About what?

PEGGY. I'm not sure. I couldn't really make it all out, but I heard him say the word "SHMUCK" a couple of times so I think it must have been about one of us.

FRANK. Why would they call *you* a shmuck?

PEGGY. That's what I thought.

FRANK. Well, they've got a lot of growing up to do. They expect everything to go their way.

PEGGY. It's a nice positive attitude.

FRANK. It's not realistic. Most things don't work out.

PEGGY. Like what?

FRANK. Just most things.

PEGGY. I want a list. I'm not letting you get away with

any more mysterious statements.

FRANK. All right. Take this weekend. You can't tell me this weekend worked out.

PEGGY. I don't think it was so bad.

FRANK. No? Well, I do. The last thing I wanted was to be picked on.

PEGGY. You think they picked on you?

FRANK. Not just they.

PEGGY. Me?

FRANK. I didn't see you stick up for me very much.

PEGGY. Why should I when I think you're wrong?

FRANK. Well, I think that's a pretty damn impersonal attitude. I'm your husband. You're my wife. We're both Virgos. I would stick up for you.

PEGGY. Even if I was wrong?

FRANK. Even if you were wrong.

PEGGY. When was I wrong?

FRANK. You were wrong not to stick up for me when I was wrong.

PEGGY. It's wrong to stick up for someone who's wrong.

FRANK. Not if he's wrong because he's misunderstood, picked on and tormented.

PEGGY. You're just feeling sorry for yourself.

FRANK. Yes, and I like it and deserve it. Thank God I've got a friend in me.

PEGGY. You know, Frank, maybe that's what you need.

FRANK. What?

PEGGY. A good friend.

FRANK. I thought you were my good friend.

PEGGY. I am. But I mean a male friend. Someone you can talk to about things you don't want to talk to me about.

FRANK. Like what?

PEGGY. Like anything. Maybe about me, our life together, your fantasies.

FRANK. I have no fantasies. It's a dog-eat-dog world and that's that. Besides, I have plenty of friends.

PEGGY. No, you don't.

FRANK. Sure I do.

PEGGY. Name-one.

FRANK. My partner.

PEGGY. You hardly speak to him.

FRANK. That's why we're friends. And what about my brothers?

PEGGY. Relatives are not friends. They're in a different category. More like the CIA. I mean, someone you can feel free to tell whatever's on your mind.

FRANK. Sure, I tell him, he tells his wife, his wife tells you and then you know what you say you don't want to know and you're waiting for me when I get home. Look, what the hell is this all about anyway?

PEGGY. Nothing, Frank. It's just that I think it's healthy for a person to have a third party to talk to. When I want to talk about certain things, I talk to Linda Hobin.

FRANK. That's good. She's a nice person. I hate her husband, though. You know, I honestly think he's taught his dog to dump on our lawn.

PEGGY. Linda's a good friend. She tells me everything and I tell her everything.

FRANK. That's terrific. I'm very happy for you.

PEGGY. When I say everything, I mean everything.

FRANK. Fine. *(interested)* Like what everything?

PEGGY. About the children, your business...

FRANK. *(relieved)* Oh.

PEGGY. Our sex life.

FRANK. *(upset)* You talk about our sex life?

PEGGY. Yes.

FRANK. What do you tell her?

PEGGY. I told you. Everything.

FRANK. Well, thank God, there's not that much to tell.
No wonder she always has a smile on her face when she
sees me. Does she tell you about her sex life?

PEGGY. Yes.

FRANK. How is it compared to ours?

PEGGY. About the same.

FRANK. You see. No one's life is perfect.

PEGGY. Frank, our problem is not sex.

FRANK. No?

PEGGY. No.

FRANK. What a relief.

*(The bedroom door opens, and TONY and JILL come out. They
carry their bags and obviously are planning to leave. FRANK and
PEGGY are surprised.)*

PEGGY. *(uneasily)* Good morning.

TONY. Good morning.

FRANK. You're packed.

JILL. Tony wants to leave.

FRANK. Gee, that's too bad. Anything wrong?

TONY. Come on, Frank. Don't hand us that crap. You

want us to go.

FRANK. *(smuggly)* No, no, I don't. *(to PEGGY)* Do I want
them to leave, Peg?

PEGGY. I think you do.

TONY. See, I knew it.

PEGGY. I enjoyed having you here. I thought it worked
out kind of nice. For the first time since I can remember,
I watched Frank behave differently. Not much, but just
enough to be encouraging.

JILL. You mean he's worse at home?

FRANK. I am wonderful at home. I'm hardly ever
there. And I would have been wonderful up here, too, if
not for a couple of young smart asses in this room whose
names I won't mention.

TONY. Frank, just what the hell do you really know
about Jill and me, anyway? It's obvious that you've made
certain judgments but what the hell do you really know
about us?

FRANK. I know a lot of things. You can tell a lot about
people without really knowing them.

TONY. You think so, huh?

FRANK. You're damn right. I know George Wash-
ington had his act together and I know Attilla The Hun
didn't. I also know you're a spoiled, cocky kid who happened to luck out with a rich old man.

TONY. Right!

FRANK. On your own you would have fallen on
your ass.

TONY. Right!

PEGGY. Come on, Frank...

FRANK. He wanted to hear it. I'm just telling him. *(to*

TONY) You have no drive! No big ambition!

TONY. Right!

FRANK. And I'll tell you something else. Without money you'd never get a girl like Jill to live with you because, in my opinion, you're not that great.

TONY. Right!

FRANK. What do you mean, right? What the hell kind of attitude is that? I said some terrible things. Aren't you going to get angry, yell, scream, fight back?

TONY. *(calmly)* Nope.

FRANK. Why "nope"?

TONY. Because my five years of analysis worked, Frank. Everything you said about me is true. I admit it, and I've learned to live with it very well.

FRANK. Goddamnit! What's the sense talking to him? Besides having it made, the lucky son-of-a-bitch is happy about it, too.

TONY. You see, Frank, I know who I am, what I am. I make no bones about it. I mean, I could make myself crazy with a lot of those things you just mentioned, but what's the sense? These are the best years of my life. I realize that. So I've worked it out with myself to be sane now, enjoy myself, and then if I have to get crazy, I'll do it later in life like when I'm your age and it obviously doesn't matter so much.

FRANK. *(to Peggy)* Does that sound like a mentally healthy person to you? That's not a mentally healthy person.

TONY. Wait a minute, Frank. I never said I was mentally healthy. Adjusted, yes, but mentally healthy, that's another thing. I happen to think mental health is a thing of the past.

FRANK. Sure. Because you young people make every-body coo-coo. *(to JILL)* Don't you have anything to say?

JILL. At this point it's safer to listen.

TONY. You are right about one thing, Frank. You can tell a lot about people without really knowing them. I can tell a lot about you. A lot more than you think.

PEGGY. Here it comes. I knew it. He's going to get you, Frank. And it's only fair.

FRANK. *(skeptical)* You can tell a lot about me?

PEGGY. Anyone want some coffee? Maybe we should all have some coffee first. Better yet, a tall glass of bourbon.

TONY. I've got you sized up in a nutshell, Frank.

FRANK. *(to TONY)* You think so.

TONY. Try me.

JILL. Tony, don't...

FRANK. *(to TONY)* You're on.

TONY. First of all, you're a schmuck, Frank.

PEGGY. See, I knew I heard the word. I'm having a drink. I'll start with beer and work my way up to arsenic. *(She gets a beer.)*

JILL. Tony, I think we should go now.

TONY. Not 'til I'm finished. *(to FRANK)* You're nothing more than an average middle-age turkey going the way of all average middle-age turkeys. You're boring and you're bored. You come home from work and you throw your-self in front of the television set. You go to bed and you put on television.

FRANK. So far, lucky guesses.

TONY. You haven't done a goddamn exciting thing in your life except, maybe once in a while when you're out of town, cheat in your hotel room.

FRANK. Peggy, pretend you didn't hear that.

TONY. Life has kicked the crap out of you, Frank, and you've accepted it. You don't hold your wife's hand anymore, you don't tell her you love her, you don't open the car door for her anymore, and you wear flannel pajamas to bed almost all year round. As far as you're concerned, Frank, the important part of your life is over.

FRANK. Oh, yeah? *(a beat)* So what?

PEGGY. What do you mean, so what?

FRANK. What makes him think he's so goddamn much better off than me?

TONY. I am, Frank, because I'm not letting life pass me by. I am not letting life slip through my fingers. I am going to enjoy myself every minute of the day. I am going to smell the roses and enjoy the sunshine and when it's all over, Frank, I won't feel short changed like you.

FRANK. *(to PEGGY)* He's burying himself, you know that?

TONY. It's what I know I want out of life, Frank. I'll never end up like you. Boring, Frank, settled, Frank, dull, Frank, lost, Frank, finished, Frank.

PEGGY. Frank, if there's a white flag around here, I suggest you raise it.

FRANK. Listen, I don't give a damn what these two say or what they think. Fifteen years from now, I guarantee you, handsome, beautiful young Tony and Jill are going to be just as boring, as settled, dull Frank and Peggy.

TONY. You think so?

FRANK. You're damn right. It's the rules of the game, my friend, the facts of life. Everybody ends up just like everybody else one day. Everybody! It's the law of the jungle. *(to PEGGY)* Right, Honey?

PEGGY. Frank.

FRANK. What?

PEGGY. Have a beer. *(She pours the beer she was drinking on FRANK'S head.)*

FRANK. Hey, what was that for?

PEGGY. *(Sets down the glass and crosses to the door.)* It's in lieu of shooting you. *(She exits. JILL hands FRANK a dish towel.)*

FRANK. *(trying to dry himself)* Now, wait, Peg! ... You don't understand again! *(turning on TONY and JILL)* Now look what you've done. I know that woman. She won't talk to me for a whole day. I hope you're happy.

TONY. Can I give you some good advice, Frank?

FRANK. No! Our marriage was like a fine piece of machinery. Just going along great. Then you two came along, and...

TONY. That's just like you, Frank. All heart and soul. Comparing a relationship to a piece of machinery.

FRANK. I'm not comparing a relationship to a piece of machinery. That's the difference. You two have a relationship. Peggy and I had a marriage. Look, I said "had". I meant "have". Oh, God, you make me nuts. Have? Had? Who cares? It's all words. Damn it, don't you think everyone would want another crack at it, at being younger than springtime and all that jazz? But you don't get another crack, not together anyway. Maybe if Peggy and I each found someone else, maybe then it could be more exciting again, or seem more exciting.

Maybe it would be just what you two have, fresh, new, adventurous ... but I don't want anyone else. I want Peggy.

JILL. That's beautiful. That's really beautiful.

FRANK. I know. But Peggy wants all that hugging and kissing crap.

JILL. Sometimes you make it very difficult to be impressed with you, Frank.

FRANK. That's only because you're immature. You two may think what we got going isn't much, but take my word for it, most of our friends think it's the best marriage on our block. *(He throws the towel at TONY and exits.)*

JILL. *(a beat)* You're not the least bit sorry, are you?

TONY. Sorry? For what? What did I do?

JILL. You were a bit rough on him. The thing about cheating in hotel rooms. You don't know if he did or not.

TONY. He lives in the suburbs. All guys who live in the suburbs cheat. It's something they do so they don't have to go home in rush hour traffic.

JILL. It was a cheap shot, and you made Peggy feel bad.

TONY. I was just retaliating for the awful things Frank said to me.

JILL. Maybe you asked for it.

TONY. Well, so did he, so we're even. Now let's just forget this whole weekend and go home.

JILL. No.

TONY. What do you mean no?

JILL. I just don't think we should go yet.

TONY. Look, I have just been through the worst few days I've ever spent in my life.

JILL. And I feel just the opposite.

TONY. You mean you had a good time?

JILL. I had an enlightened time.

TONY. Too bad. That's no way to spend a holiday.

JILL. Tony, how much of your life would you like to spend with me?

TONY. Oh, Christ.

JILL. I'm asking you a simple question.

TONY. It's a dumb question.

JILL. Not to me.

TONY. A thousand years, a million years...

JILL. I'd like you to be more specific.

TONY. You're feeling insecure, right?

JILL. Right.

TONY. All the carrying on this weekend has given you a lot of fears and doubts about us, right?

JILL. Right.

TONY. You're convinced that we're gonna end up in the same rut as Peggy and Frank, and it's got you frightened to death, right?

JILL. Wrong!

TONY. Wrong?

JILL. I'm not sure we're going to end up like them and that's the problem.

TONY. I don't get it.

JILL. Tony, I want you to marry me.

TONY. *(A beat. Stunned.)* Maybe we should talk about sports. How about those Mets, huh? They won two in a row.

JILL. Screw the Mets. I want you to marry me.

TONY. For God's sake, why?

JILL. Because I love you.

TONY. What kind of reason is that?

JILL. Because you love me?

TONY. You're talking in circles. Just what the hell do you see in a relationship like Frank and Peggy's that you find so damn attractive?

JILL. Commitment.

TONY. Okay, I'll commit you.

JILL. You don't want to make a commitment to me, do you?

TONY. What the hell kind of talk is that? I thought our love for each other was supposed to be commitment enough. I thought our mutual respect and understanding was a commitment. I thought sending our laundry out together was a commitment.

JILL. Stop ranting. We are having a discussion.

TONY. You are having a discussion. I am having an anxiety attack.

JILL. I don't want us to ever stop loving each other, Tony.

TONY. Neither do I. But why do we have to sign a paper to prove it?

JILL. Because everything changes, Tony, even love. I love you, Tony. No matter what happens to us, what difficulties we go through, I don't want it to be too easy for either of us to walk away.

TONY. And that's why we should get married?

JILL. Yes.

TONY. Look, can we finish this conversation in the car?

I'll drive a hundred miles an hour. It'll take your mind off of everything.

JILL. I want to know that you belong to me. That I can tell you off or pour a beer on your head, that at times you can be a complete jerk and that some mornings I can wake up nasty as hell and it's not going to make either of us quit.

TONY. And that's why we should get married?

JILL. Yes. I want to know that years from now, we'll still need each other as much as Peggy and Frank do.

TONY. You're getting your period, right? You always talk crazy a couple of days before you have your period. *(relieved)* Thank God you're getting your period. For a while I thought we were really in trouble.

JILL. I'm not getting my period. Let's face it, Tony. This is the way it had to end up no matter what we planned or promised at the start.

TONY. End up? Why does there always have to be an end, a goddamn button on everything? A finish? Why can't we just go along with things as if they're never going to end?

JILL. Beause they do. There are a lot of finishes in life. You finish being an infant. You finish being a teenager. You finish being the beautiful people that we are trying so hard to be. Marry me, Tony.

TONY. Can I get back to you in a couple of days?

JILL. No. I want an answer now and I'm not leaving till I get one.

TONY. I .. I don't ... I can't .. I...

JILL. That sounds like no, doesn't it?

TONY. No, it's not no.

JILL. *(hopefully)* Then it's yes?

TONY. No, it's not yes either. Is there such a thing as yes and no?

JILL. Maybe.

TONY. Yes! That's it! Maybe!

JILL. I can't accept maybe.

TONY. No?

JILL. Yes. *(TONY picks up a suitcase.)* Look, I'm leaving here. If you want to come, okay.

JILL. Fine. *(She sits down.)*

TONY. Really?

JILL. Uh huh?

TONY. Are you sure?

JILL. Positive.

TONY. I'm warning you.

JILL. I'm warned.

TONY. Goodbye.

JILL. So long.

TONY. I'm going.

JILL. See you. *(TONY goes to the door, looks at her. JILL doesn't move. TONY sighs and drops his suitcase.)*

SLOW FADE

Scene Two

Time:Several hours later.

JILL, wiping the kitchen table off, calmly watches TONY as he nervously paces the room just the way FRANK did. TONY goes to the window, looks out for a few beats and then returns to his pacing.

JILL. Maybe you should go out and look for them.

TONY. Where am I going to look? They could have gone off in fifteen different directions. They'll be okay.

JILL. I don't think it's like Frank to miss lunch.

TONY. He probably hasn't. I don't care where you go in this country, eventually you run into a McDonald's. Anyway, they're big people. We don't have to worry about them. Look, I'd like to leave now. If it gets much later, it'll be too dark to drive these roads and I'm not spending another night here under any circumstances. If I want to see a couple having difficulties I'll go and visit my parents.

JILL. I told you I wasn't going.

TONY. You told me that two hours ago. I thought by now you forgot.

JILL. A woman never forgets.

TONY. That's an elephant who never forgets.

JILL. Well, a woman never forgets even longer. Why are you having such a hard time deciding whether you want to marry me or not?

TONY. Because I wasn't prepared to make this decision now.

JILL. When do you think you will be?

TONY. I don't know. But not now. Maybe when I start to lose my hair.

JILL. I think what you're going through is known as the moment of truth.

TONY. What I'm going through is known as the moment of terror. As long as I live I will never understand women.

JILL. That's good. We need the edge.

TONY. What if we went to see a counselor.

JILL. We will. As soon as our marriage is in trouble. I promise.

TONY. I wouldn't be surprised if you planned to do this to me all along.

JILL. Frankly, I'm a little disappointed that I didn't.

(FRANK and PEGGY enter. FRANK'S right pant leg is wrinkled.)

FRANK. I was hoping you wouldn't be here.

TONY. So was I.

FRANK. It's nothing personal. It's just that at this point in time I'm not too thrilled with you.

TONY. It seems to be the trend. *(to JILL)* Come on, Jill. Let's go home.

JILL. No. Not until you give me an answer.

TONY. It isn't fair!

JILL. Fairness is not the issue.

PEGGY. Frank, we missed an issue. Quick, what is it?

TONY. The whole system of male and female relationships ... It doesn't work. In this world there should be either all men or all women.

FRANK. That's dumb. If there were no women, who

would you get to take the kid's to school?

TONY. I'm not turning into you, Frank. I want everyone in this room to know right here and now. I am not ever going to be like you ... *(indicates JILL)* And that's the way she'd like me to be, too.

FRANK. *(impressed)* She would? You hear that, Peggy? She'd like him to be like me. Maybe I'm not such a bad guy after all. *(to JILL)* Why do you want him to be like me?

TONY. Come on, Honey. It's getting late. Let's go home. We can talk about this later.

FRANK. No, no. I gotta hear this.

JILL. I'm not going anywhere with you, Tony, until you promise to marry me.

TONY. Promise to marry you? What happened to yes, no and maybe?

JILL. I'm trying to make it easier for you. I don't think you can handle all those choices.

FRANK. Excuse me, but can you run that by us one more time.

TONY. Marry her! She wants me to marry her!

FRANK. *(thrilled)* Hear that, Peg? He's getting the screws put to him, too. No one gets away with murder forever.

TONY. *(to JILL)* I don't understand you. *(indicates FRANK and PEGGY)* Their life will not work for us. It's barely working for them. I mean ... what the hell do you think you're going to get out of something like this?

PEGGY. I'll be interested in this one.

JILL. I just want to know that when I reach fifty or sixty, there will be somebody around ... to want me ... to need me.

FRANK. Who the hell's sixty?

PEGGY. Me! I've aged since I've been up here!

JILL. This weekend with you two showed me how great it is to have someone be your friend always, to share the good times and the bad. Someone to get old with, gain weight with and get wrinkled with.

FRANK. That's the worst commercial for marriage I ever heard.

PEGGY. Maybe you'd like to know why we were gone so long. I was very upset when I left and Frank wanted to calm me down. He asked me to go for a walk with him, so I did. He put his arm around me and we went down to that little lake you told us about. We didn't talk much, hardly at all. We just went down there and began throwing stones in the water just the way you said you did.

JILL. And?

PEGGY. And Frank fell in the water.

TONY. Tough crackers, Frank...

FRANK. I don't need your sympathy.

PEGGY. Anyway, it made me laugh. I laughed, and laughed and laughed.

FRANK. I didn't find it funny. I think I ruined these pants, and they go with every shirt I own.

PEGGY. It just made me realize that Frank is Frank. He isn't going to change and you know something, he doesn't have to. I'm afraid he's mine for better or worse.

FRANK. That's sweet. Isn't that sweet?

JILL. It is, isn't it, Tony? It is.

TONY. Who cares?

FRANK. *(to PEGGY)* I know I'm not as romantic as I

used to be, if I ever used to be, but I do love you, Peg. Maybe I don't say it as often as I should, but you know I do. I mean, there's no one else I want to live with the rest of my life. Isn't that love?

PEGGY. Maybe it is, Frank. And maybe I do love you because I worry about you. I worry about you when you come home with a cold and when your business upsets you. I worry about you when you have to take an airplane trip. You and I belong to each other, and whether it's love or whatever, we need each other and we're still better off together than apart.

FRANK. Hear that! Hear that! *(to TONY)* That's what we got!

TONY. So what?

FRANK. So what? So I guess I'm a happily married man after all. Now it's your move.

TONY. Let's go, Jill.

JILL. I'm still waiting for an answer.

TONY. This time I mean it. I'm not staying.

JILL. And I mean it too. I'm waiting.

FRANK. Hold it! Hold it! Time out! Don't move, any-one. *(All eyes look at him curiously as he rushes to the cupboard.)*

PEGGY. I hope this is going to be something you won't regret, Frank.

FRANK. Don't worry. *(Taking out the box of Cocoa Puffs, he rushes back and sits between TONY and JILL.)* Okay, now where were we? She wants to get married and he wants to go home. Lights, camera, action. *(FRANK starts eating the cereal.)*

SLOW FADE

Scene Three

Time: Monday morning. PEGGY is at an open suitcase. Another one of their suitcases is nearby.

Everything is neat and put away. A camera and a box of groceries are on the table.

The front door opens and TONY enters.

TONY. *(calling)* Jill!
JILL. *(offstage)* Coming!
PEGGY. She's just fixing her hair.
TONY. *(Notices camera on table. He brings it to her.)* Don't forget your camera.
PEGGY. I won't.
TONY. Did you take any pictures?
PEGGY. No.
TONY. That's too bad.
PEGGY. I have a feeling it was for the best. I'm not so sure Frank can take the memories.

(FRANK enters front door.)

FRANK. I got most of the food in the trunk. We've still got enough stuff to last for a month.
PEGGY. That's the marvelous thing about tension. It curbs your appetite.

(JILL comes out of the bedroom with a bag.)

JILL. I'm ready. You know, we never left this early before.

TONY. I just think we'd better. After a weekend like this, I have to go home to rest up.

JILL. Whatever you say. *(takes TONY'S hand)* Well, Tony, another year.

TONY. *(lacklustre)* Uh-huh, another year.

JILL. Come on. Show a little enthusiasm.

TONY. *(same tone)* Uh-huh, another year.

JILL. Much better.

TONY. Look, Frank, next Memorial Day you can have this place all to yourselves. I think from now on, I'm spending all my holidays in my closet.

JILL. Actually, I think this whole weekend was like group therapy.

FRANK. Who needed it? I was completely normal until I came up here.

JILL. I think we came to some wonderful conclusions. One, that Peggy and Frank are happily married, an two ... that Tony and I soon will be.

FRANK. I'm still laughing about the last part. Ha ha!

TONY. Ha ha, your ass.

FRANK. He's upset. I love it!

TONY. Sure, I'm upset. Getting married is a big step in a man's life. But the funny thing is, I'm not sorry. I mean, I never thought I would, but I am. And once I said I would, I knew I meant it. And once I knew I meant it, I felt glad. And once I felt glad, I knew I was trapped. And once I felt trapped, I felt upset because why should a guy feel glad about being trapped unless he wanted to get married all along which would upset anyone, no matter how confused he was. The truth is, Jill, I love you. I really do. I guess we would have been married sooner or later. This just made it sooner, so what's the big deal.

PEGGY. You know, Frank, there's a lot of you in every man.

FRANK. Thank you.

TONY. But one thing our marriage is not going to do is change our life style. We're still going to take trips and go out a lot and have fun. Actually, everything's going to be just the same.

JILL. Absolutely. We might need a bigger apartment later on when we have children, but, outside of that, nothing will really change, except maybe we can replace some of your awful old furniture and that dangerous mirror on the bedroom ceiling.

TONY. I'm sick.

FRANK. Who the hell puts a mirror on the ceiling?

TONY. You wouldn't understand.

PEGGY. Well, good luck to both of you. And keep us posted.

JILL. Of course we will. You'll come to the wedding.

PEGGY. We'd love to!

TONY. Actually, it'll probably be a small, intimate affair.

JILL. Oh, no. I made out the guest list. It came to two hundred and fifty people.

TONY. Guest list? What guest list?

JILL. While you were thinking it over, I made out the

guest list.

PEGGY. Now that's confidence.

JILL. I knew I had him when I heard him crying in the bathroom. *(FRANK laughs tauntingly.)*

TONY. *(sadly)* It's the first time I cried in years.

FRANK. And it's only the beginning.

JILL. Well, we'd better be on our way. *(She kisses FRANK and PEGGY on the cheek.)* Goodbye. It was fabulous.

PEGGY. It was wonderful.

TONY. It was great.

FRANK. It was so-so. That's the best I can offer.

TONY. *(kisses PEGGY)* Call you in the city, Frank. *(They ad lib final goodbyes. "Be good. Careful driving down the hill..." TONY and JILL exit.)*

FRANK. Well, there they go.

PEGGY. There they go.

FRANK. *(beat)* Boy, I'm glad we're not them. I really mean it this time. It's not easy being young anymore. You have too much future to face. I don't think I could stand to go through it again.

PEGGY. Of course, you could, Frank. You're a terrific human being.

FRANK. Maybe. You know, we'll probably never see them again.

PEGGY. You think not?

FRANK. I know not. They never took our number.

PEGGY. They could get it from Information.

FRANK. They wouldn't know what suburb. They didn't ask where we lived.

PEGGY. Tony could get you through the company.

FRANK. Yeah, I guess so ... if he wanted to. But I don't

think he will.

PEGGY. If they don't call, they don't call.

FRANK. I just hate being handed a line. If a guy meets you, seems to kind of like you, talks about inviting you to his wedding and says he'll call you in the city, there should be some sincerity there.

PEGGY. You sound like a jilted woman.

FRANK. Well, it's annoying.

PEGGY. I think it's just as well if they don't call us. They were much too young for us anyway. We'd probably feel more comfortable around people our own age.

FRANK. Maybe. if we want to hang around young people, we can always go to dinner with our kids. At least we know, up front, they're out to get us. *(He takes a bag to the door and places it outside.)*

PEGGY. I think they really did like us, though. I do.

FRANK. You do?

PEGGY. Yes.

FRANK. Well, then, I guess they weren't so bad, either. Everything all cleaned up?

PEGGY. Yes. *(She picks up a bag. FRANK picks up the last box of groceries. They are at opposite ends of the stage.)*

FRANK. Okay. Let's go.

PEGGY. *(a beat)* Frank?

FRANK. What?

PEGGY. I'm sorry for some of the things I said.

FRANK. Yeah, me too. But we did say a few things that made sense.

PEGGY. That's true.

FRANK. Like what?

PEGGY. That we need each other.

FRANK. Yeah, it's probably good for couples to remind themselves of that every now and then.

PEGGY. I guess that alone is worth it.

FRANK. You bet. Look, if you want to come up here again, I mean, try it again, just the two of us, I will.

PEGGY. Maybe someday.

FRANK. Yeah, we talked, we said things ... so what if it almost wrecked out marriage? ... You know, maybe I really have been taking you too much for granted.

PEGGY. No. No, you've been very fair.

FRANK. I thought so. Well, let's go. *(They start out.)* I wonder what the hell's happening in the world. I miss not having anything to complain about.

PEGGY. I hope Linda watered my plants. The last time I left town, the rubber trees turned blue.

FRANK. I thought they looked better that way. Everyone' got green plants.

PEGGY. *(offstage)* Don't forget to leave the key under the mat.

FRANK. Right. *(He puts the key under the mat and is about to close the door. He looks around one more time.)* Well, so long cabin. So long sofa. So long fireplace, tables, chairs. It's been a hell of an experience. *(a beat)* **Peggy!** *(louder)* **Peggy!**

PEGGY. *(off)* **What!**

FRANK. Get back here. We're staying! *(FRANK puts the box of groceries back on the table.)*

(PEGGY enters.)

PEGGY. Staying?

FRANK. The hell with the business, the hell with the kids, the hell with everything. We've got enough chicken, I've got plenty of sweaters, we're staying up here three more days.

PEGGY. Frank, have you had a stroke?

FRANK. Who cares? Just lock the door. We don't need any more visitors.

PEGGY. *(locks the door)* Right.

FRANK. Where were we before we were interrupted?

PEGGY. Well, I was on the floor and you were telling me all the places we were going to make love. On the sofa, on the table...

FRANK. That's right. And do you know what we're going to do when we finish?

PEGGY. What?

FRANK. We're going to go for a walk again and I'm going to hold your hand and kiss your ear, and we're going to go down to that little lake and throw stones in the water and this time I'm not falling in. What do you think of that? *(He starts kissing her on the cheek tenderly.)*

PEGGY. *(tenderly)* Frank?

FRANK. Huh?

PEGGY. I've always loved you, you know that?

FRANK. Honey, how could you help it. *(They kiss and sink to the floor.)*

FINAL CURTAIN

COSTUME PLOT

FRANK

ACT I — SCENE 1
Dark brown pants
Light brown T-shirt
Brown topsiders

SCENE 2
T-shirt (same)
Shoes and socks (same)
Brown warm up suit

SCENE 3
Same as Scene 2

ACT II — SCENE 1
Grey warm up suit
Shoes (same)

SCENE 2
Grey sweater
White shirt
Blue pants
Shoes (same)

PEGGY

ACT I — SCENE 1
Black peignoir
Black slippers

SCENE 2
Red housecoat worn over peignoir from Scene 1

SCENE 3
Flowered caftan

ACT II — SCENE 1
Another matching housecoat and slippers

SCENE 2
Same as Scene 1

SCENE 3
Skirt
Blouse
Cardigan sweater
Shoes and nylons

TONY

ACT I — SCENE 1
Stripped shirt
Crew neck sweater
Black dress pants
Black loafers

SCENE 2
White sweatshirt
Blue jeans
Sweat socks
White sneakers

SCENE 3
Same as Scene 2

ACT II — SCENE 1
Same as Act I — Scene 1

SCENE 2
Same as Act I — Scene 1

SCENE 3
Sweater over same pants as in above scenes

JILL

ACT I — SCENE 1
Tight fitting black slacks
Black shoes
Pink sweater

SCENE 2
Blue jeans
Light blue T-shirt with collar
White sneakers

SCENE 3
Same as Scene 2
Add white sweatshirt to match Tony's

ACT II — SCENE 1
Same pants and shoes as in Act I, Scene 1.
Add yellow sweater

SCENE 2
Same as Act II, Scene 1

SCENE 3
A different tight fitting slack and sweater outfit
Appropriate shoes

PROP LIST

BASIC SET
   Sofa bed
   Coffee table
   Easy chair
   Lamp table
   Table lamp
   Kitchen table
   Four kitchen chairs
   Linen chest
   Refrigerator (well stocked, eggs, bread, OJ)
   Counter stove and sink
   Fireplace equipment
   Several logs
   Curtains on windows
   Coffee pot, toaster, frying pan
   Drinking glasses, coffee cups, plates
   Six beers in refrigerator

ACT I, SCENE 1
Pre set
   Large suit case
   Three boxes of groceries
      (containing 4 boxes of various breakfast cereals)

Props brought in
   Several logs (Frank)
   Two suit cases (Tony and Jill)
   Tape player (Tony)
   Coin (Tony)
   Bottles of champagne (Tony)

ACT I, SCENE 2
Pre set on table
        Six empty tin foil trays
        Four champagne glasses
        Kitchen utensils (plastic)
        Crumpled napkins
        Large plastic trash bag
        Set of car keys

Props brought on
        Two five-dollar bills (Frank)
        One ten-dollar bill (Tony)

ACT I, SCENE 3
        Knitting utensils (Peggy)
        Paperback book (Tony)

ACT II, SCENE 1
        Large kitchen towel (pre set)

ACT II, SCENE 3
        Camera and case

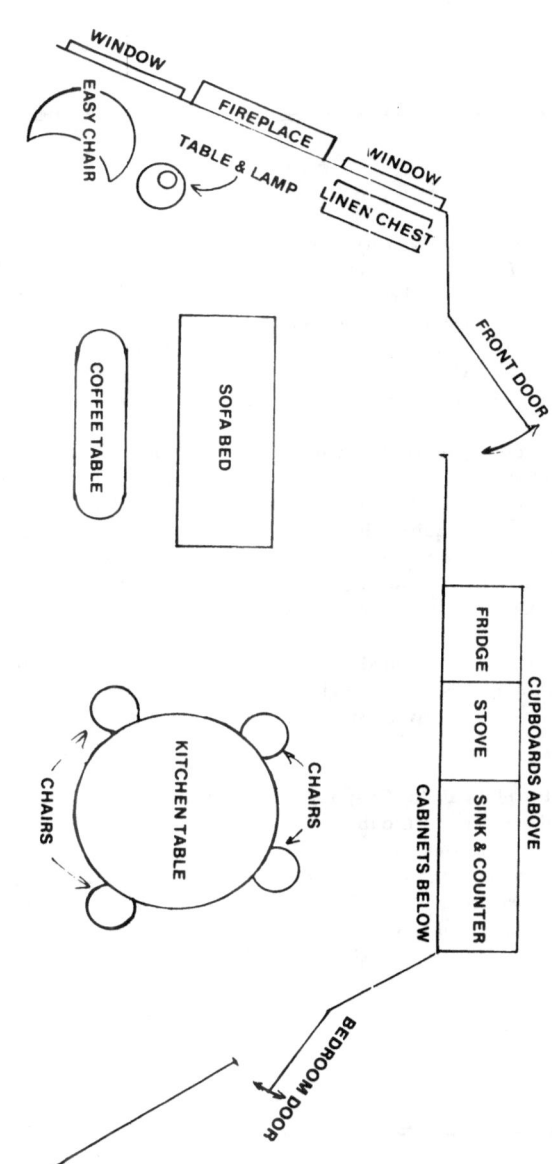

WINDOW

EASY CHAIR

FIREPLACE

WINDOW

TABLE & LAMP

LINEN CHEST

FRONT DOOR

COFFEE TABLE

SOFA BED

FRIDGE

STOVE

SINK & COUNTER

CUPBOARDS ABOVE

CABINETS BELOW

KITCHEN TABLE

CHAIRS

CHAIRS

BEDROOM DOOR

CABIN
WEEKEND COMEDY
BASIC SET

SKIN DEEP
Jon Lonoff

Comedy / 2m, 2f / Interior Unit Set

In *Skin Deep*, a large, lovable, lonely-heart, named Maureen Mulligan, gives romance one last shot on a blind-date with sweet awkward Joseph Spinelli; she's learned to pepper her speech with jokes to hide insecurities about her weight and appearance, while he's almost dangerously forthright, saying everything that comes to his mind. They both know they're perfect for each other, and in time they come to admit it.

They were set up on the date by Maureen's sister Sheila and her husband Squire, who are having problems of their own: Sheila undergoes a non-stop series of cosmetic surgeries to hang onto the attractive and much-desired Squire, who may or may not have long ago held designs on Maureen, who introduced him to Sheila. With Maureen particularly vulnerable to both hurting and being hurt, the time is ripe for all these unspoken issues to bubble to the surface.

"Warm-hearted comedy ... the laughter was literally show-stopping. A winning play, with enough good-humored laughs and sentiment to keep you smiling from beginning to end."
- TalkinBroadway.com

"It's a little Paddy Chayefsky, a lot Neil Simon and a quick-witted, intelligent voyage into the not-so-tranquil seas of middle-aged love and dating. The dialogue is crackling and hilarious; the plot simple but well-turned; the characters endearing and quirky; and lurking beneath the merriment is so much heartache that you'll stand up and cheer when the unlikely couple makes it to the inevitable final clinch."
- NYTheatreWorld.Com

THE OFFICE PLAYS
Two full length plays by Adam Bock

THE RECEPTIONIST
Comedy / 2m, 2f / Interior
At the start of a typical day in the Northeast Office, Beverly deals effortlessly with ringing phones and her colleague's romantic troubles. But the appearance of a charming rep from the Central Office disrupts the friendly routine. And as the true nature of the company's business becomes apparent, The Receptionist raises disquieting, provocative questions about the consequences of complicity with evil.

"...Mr. Bock's poisoned Post-it note of a play."
- New York Times

"Bock's intense initial focus on the routine goes to the heart of
The Receptionist's pointed, painfully timely allegory... elliptical,
provocative play..."
- Time Out New York

THE THUGS
Comedy / 2m, 6f / Interior
The Obie Award winning dark comedy about work, thunder and the mysterious things that are happening on the 9th floor of a big law firm. When a group of temps try to discover the secrets that lurk in the hidden crevices of their workplace, they realize they would rather believe in gossip and rumors than face dangerous realities.

"Bock starts you off giggling, but leaves you with a chill."
- Time Out New York

"... a delightfully paranoid little nightmare that is both more
chillingly realistic and pointedly absurd than anything
John Grisham ever dreamed up."
- New York Times

BLUE YONDER
Kate Aspengren

Dramatic Comedy / Monolgues and scenes
12f (can be performed with as few as 4 with doubling) / Unit Set

A familiar adage states, "Men may work from sun to sun, but women's work is never done." In BIue Yonder, the audience meets twelve mesmerizing and eccentric women including a flight instructor, a firefighter, a stuntwoman, a woman who donates body parts, an employment counselor, a professional softball player, a surgical nurse professional baseball player, and a daredevil who plays with dynamite among others. Through the monologues, each woman examines her life's work and explores the career that she has found. Or that has found her.

WHITE BUFFALO
Don Zolidis

Drama / 3m, 2f (plus chorus)/ Unit Set

Based on actual events, WHITE BUFFALO tells the story of the miracle birth of a white buffalo calf on a small farm in southern Wisconsin. When Carol Gelling discovers that one of the buffalo on her farm is born white in color, she thinks nothing more of it than a curiosity. Soon, however, she learns that this is the fulfillment of an ancient prophecy believed by the Sioux to bring peace on earth and unity to all mankind. Her little farm is quickly overwhelmed with religious pilgrims, bringing her into contact with a culture and faith that is wholly unfamiliar to her. When a mysterious businessman offers to buy the calf for two million dollars, Carol is thrown into doubt about whether to profit from the religious beliefs of others or to keep true to a spirituality she knows nothing about.